The Lion and the Mouse
and Other Stories

Contents

igloobooks

The Lion and the Elephant

"RoarRRR!" Lion was King of the Beasts. He ruled the animal world and everyone was in **awe** of him. However, there was one animal who didn't care whether he pleased Lion or not.

That animal was a cockerel. He crowed every single morning.
The sound was so **loud** that the lion began to feel afraid
of the cockerel and the horrid noise it made.
"Go away!" cried Lion.

"COCK-A-DOODLE-DO!"

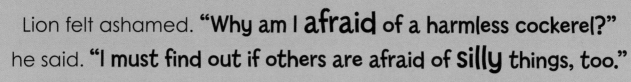

Lion felt ashamed. "Why am I **afraid** of a harmless cockerel?" he said. "I **must find out** if others are afraid of **silly** things, too." With that, Lion headed off into the jungle and came across two monkeys, who were playing in the trees.

"Monkeys, are you afraid of anything?" called out Lion.

"We get scared of being **eaten** by lions like you!" they cried.

"What about the crowing of the cockerel?" asked Lion.

"You **must** be **joking**," replied the monkeys, laughing.

HA! HA! HA! HA! HA! HA!

Lion crept away to the river. There, he saw Hippopotamus.
"Is there anything you're afraid of?" asked Lion.
"I'm afraid of crocodile **teeth**," replied Hippopotamus.
"They are **pointy** and **sharp**."

"What about the crowing of the cockerel?" asked Lion.
"You **must** be **joking**," replied Hippopotamus.

Just then, Elephant came lumbering out of the jungle.
"Can I speak to you a moment?" asked Lion.
"Not just now, I have a SERIOUS problem,"
replied Elephant, shaking his head.

"I have a **serious** problem, too," said Lion, feeling ashamed.
"Every morning when I hear the cockerel's crow, I feel afraid."
"Well, I'm afraid I'll **die** if a mosquito flies in my ear," said Elephant.

"A **mighty elephant** afraid of a tiny mosquito?" said Lion.
Suddenly, he realised how **silly** his own fear was.

"Thank you, Elephant," said Lion, brightly. "Now I know I'm not the only one with silly fears, I feel **much better.**"

The following morning, Cockerel crowed. "It's only a sound," said Lion, smiling. "It can't hurt me."

Everyone has something they are afraid of.

"COCK-A-DOODLE-DO!"

The Gnat and the Lion

One evening, deep in the savannah, the animals were getting ready to sleep. Two, however, were only just waking up. One of these was a gnat.

"This is the best time of day to go and do some stinging," said Gnat, gleefully.

The other animal was a lion. He opened his enormous jaws.
"**Roar!**" said Lion. Gnat laughed.

"you may be King of the Beasts," said Gnat,
"but you don't frighten me."

"I could **destroy** you with one **swipe** of my paw," warned Lion.
"I'd like to see you try," said Gnat.

Annoyed by Gnat's challenge, Lion swiped at him with his paw. **"Take that!"** he roared. **"You missed me!"** said Gnat, cheekily. Lion continued to bat at the gnat, twisting his head this way and that, but Gnat was simply too **quick** for him.

BuzzZz

Swish

"Keep still!" roared Lion, as Gnat flew around his body.
"Make me," taunted Gnat, who then flew straight up Lion's
nose and began to **sting** him.

"Stop!" bellowed Lion, but Gnat kept on stinging him.

Lion batted his great paws at his nose but, no matter
how hard he tried, he could not dislodge Gnat.

"Say I'm King of the Beasts," demanded Gnat.
"Never!" yelled Lion.
Gnat tugged Lion's nose hairs. **"Say it,"** he repeated.
Lion couldn't bare the pain any longer.
"Gnat is King of the Beasts!" he cried.

"**Thank you,**" said Gnat, popping out of Lion's nose.
"**I'm the smartest creature ever,**" boasted Gnat, as he flew
away from Lion. "**I think I deserve a home fit for a king!**"

Soon, Gnat saw a web draped over a bush. "**That looks perfect,**"
he said. He landed on the web and wrapped it around him.

BuzzZZ

"You're **trapped!**" cried a spider.

Gnat was scared and tried to fly away, but was caught in the web.

"How dare you," he stammered. **"I'm King of the Beasts."**

"No, you're not," said Spider, **"but I'll let you go if you're humble and admit you're just a gnat."**

Gotcha

"I'm only a gnat," he said, feebly. **"So, can you please set me free now?"** Spider released him. **"A real king wouldn't have put himself in so much danger,"** he said. **"You're right,"** replied Gnat. **"I should never have been so boastful."** Gnat had learnt his lesson and he never taunted anyone again.

Aaargh

Pride always comes before a fall.

The Lion and the Mouse

One hot afternoon, Lion was asleep. His snore was so loud that all of the animals in Africa could hear him.

"What's that **terrible** noise?" asked Ostrich.

"What's that **awful** din?" asked Baby Elephant.

"What's that **monstrous** hullabaloo?" asked Rhino.

So deep was Lion's sleep that he didn't hear a thing,
or even feel two mice running along his back.
When the mice grew tired, they sat on the lion's nose.
"That was fun," said one mouse, twitching his whiskers.
"Let's do it again," said the other, flicking his tail.

ZZZZ

The **twitching** and **flicking** woke Lion, who swiped at his nose.
One mouse dodged the blow, but the other was too slow and fell.
Lion stared at the mouse, then opened his **enormous** mouth.
"Please don't eat me!" squeaked Mouse.
"Why not?" said Lion.

"If you spare me," pleaded Mouse, "you won't regret it."
"That's a **big promise** for a little mouse," said Lion.
"If you are ever in trouble," said Mouse, "I will help you."
"Okay, I'll let you go," said Lion.
"Thank you," squeaked Mouse.

GRRRrrr

The next day, Lion was walking through the jungle when
WHOOSH! A net closed around him and pulled him up.
Lion struggled, but couldn't free himself. He **roared** in fury.

Far away, Mouse heard Lion's roar. **"Lion is in trouble!"** he cried. **"I must go and help him."** Mouse ran all day and didn't stop until he reached Lion.

"Please help me," *pleaded Lion.*

"I'll set you free," *said Mouse.*

Mouse gnawed at the net. Soon, a big hole appeared and Lion slipped through. He fell to the ground with a **THUD**.

"You saved my life," said Lion.

"Just as you once saved mine," replied Mouse.

From that day on, Lion and Mouse were the best of friends.

Never dismiss an offer of help,
no matter how small it may seem.